The box was by Chip's bed.
Something was glowing inside it.

Chip looked at the box.
'It's magic,' he said.

Chip ran into Biff's room.
'Biff,' he called.
'Look at the box.'

3

Biff and Chip looked at the box.
Something was glowing inside it.

They opened the box.
They looked inside.
'It's magic,' they said.

A key was in the box.
The key was glowing.

'It's a magic key,' said Biff.
She picked up the key and
  the magic began.

Biff and Chip got smaller and
smaller and smaller.

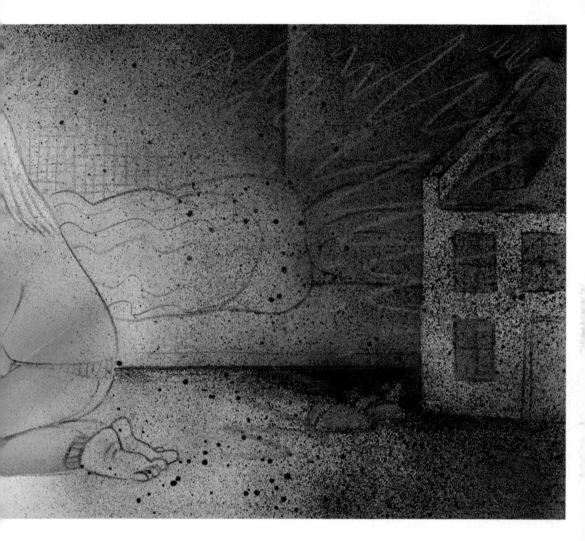

'Oh help!' said Biff.
'It's magic,' said Chip.

Biff and Chip looked at the room.
Everything looked big.

'Look at my big slippers,' said Biff.
'Everything looks big.'

Chip picked up a pencil.
'Look at this big pencil,' he said.

Biff picked up a pin.

'Look at this big pin,' she said.

They looked at the house.
It looked like a big house.

The windows were glowing.
'It's magic,' said Chip.

Biff and Chip ran to the house.
They looked in the window.

Biff went to the door.
She pushed and pushed, but
she couldn't get in.

They went to the window.
Chip pulled and pulled, but
    he couldn't get in.

Something was coming.
Chip picked up the pin.
'Oh help!' he said.

It was a little mouse.
Biff and Chip looked at the mouse.
The mouse ran away.

Something was glowing.
It was the magic key.
Biff picked it up.

Biff and Chip got bigger and
bigger and bigger.

'Oh no!' said Biff.

'Oh help!' said Chip.

'It's the magic,' they said.

The magic was over.
'What an adventure!' said Biff and Chip.